KU-740-653

To my adventurers,
Freya, Henry and Wilf
A.F.

To three very special stars in my life
Nic, Ben and Elle
xxx
L.G.

A PLACE CALLED HME

Addy Farmer and Louise Gardner

Supported using public funding by

 Department for Education | ARTS COUNCIL ENGLAND

Just past the moon,
in deep, darkest space,
there's a greeny-blue planet
and a snuggly-bug place
called home.

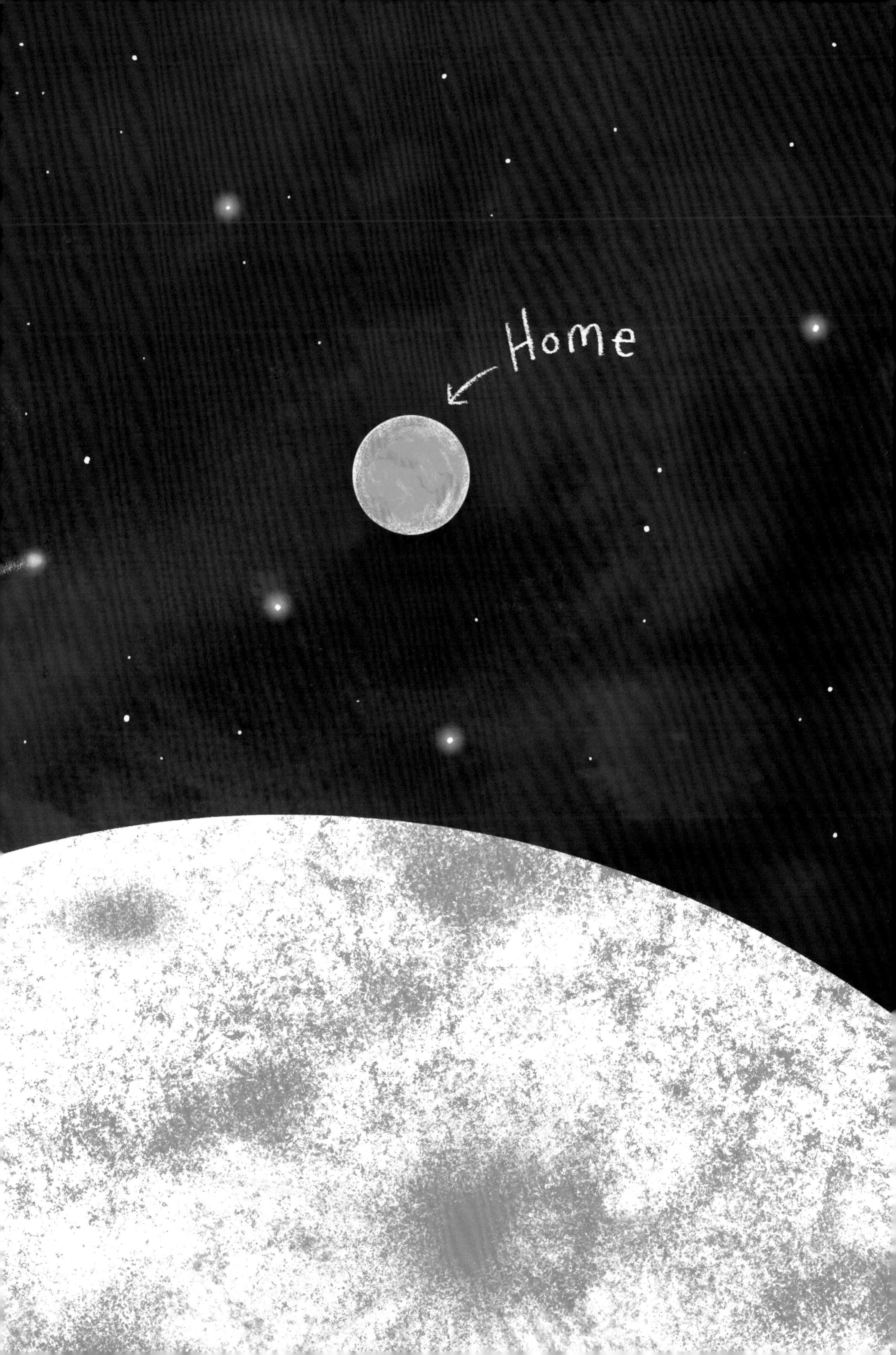
Home

"Let's explore!
Rocket ready!
Press the button...
Whee!" said Eddy.
"Whoosh!" said Freddy.
"Look!" said Blip.

One light blue-ish day
when things had to be done —
like new shoes
and hair cuts —
and nothing was fun...

They waited and waited
and waited for Mum...
Until finally
Eddy got ready
to run!

"Let's explore!
Rocket ready!
Press the button...
Whee!" said Eddy.
"Whoosh!" said Freddy.
"Whoops!" said Blip.

The engine blasted
The rocket raced UP UP UP

through the clouds
and out into space...

The rocket flew far
through a sky full of stars,
past BIG ships and SMALL ships
and pirates from Mars.

"We know what to do!"
said Eddy and Freddy.
Then straight down they flew...

"Are we home yet?" asked Blip.
"No! It's somewhere new!"

They saw Crotchety crabs and
Big Bobble fish
who bounced up and down and
blew bubbles like this...

BLUBBLE SPLUBBLE PLUBBLE

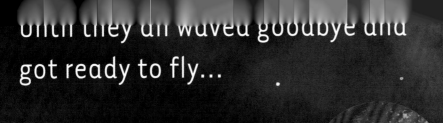

until they all waved goodbye and
got ready to fly...

"Let's explore!
Rocket ready!
Press the button...
Whee!" said Eddy.
"Whoosh!" said Freddy.
"Look," said Blip.

The rocket flew far
through a sky full of stars,
past **SLOOOW** ships and *FAST* ships
and pirates from Mars.

"We know what to do,"
said Eddy and Freddy.
Then straight down they flew...

"Are we home yet?" asked Blip.
"No! It's somewhere new!"

Frost fairies danced
on the rainbow ice ponds,
ringing and singing
their high tinkling songs...

JINGLE

TINGLE

TWINGLE

Until they all waved goodbye and
got ready to fly...

"Let's explore!
Rocket ready!
Press the button...
Whee!" said Eddy.
"Whoosh!" said Freddy.
"Look!" said Blip.

The rocket flew far
through a sky full of stars,
past **LOUD** ships and ssS**SSH!** ships
and pirates from Mars.

"We know what to do,"
said Freddy and Eddy.
Then straight down they flew...

"Are we home yet?" asked Blip.
"No! It's somewhere new!"

In the Woolly Woo's wood
they ate purple plum pie.
They laughed and played games
like chase and I-spy...

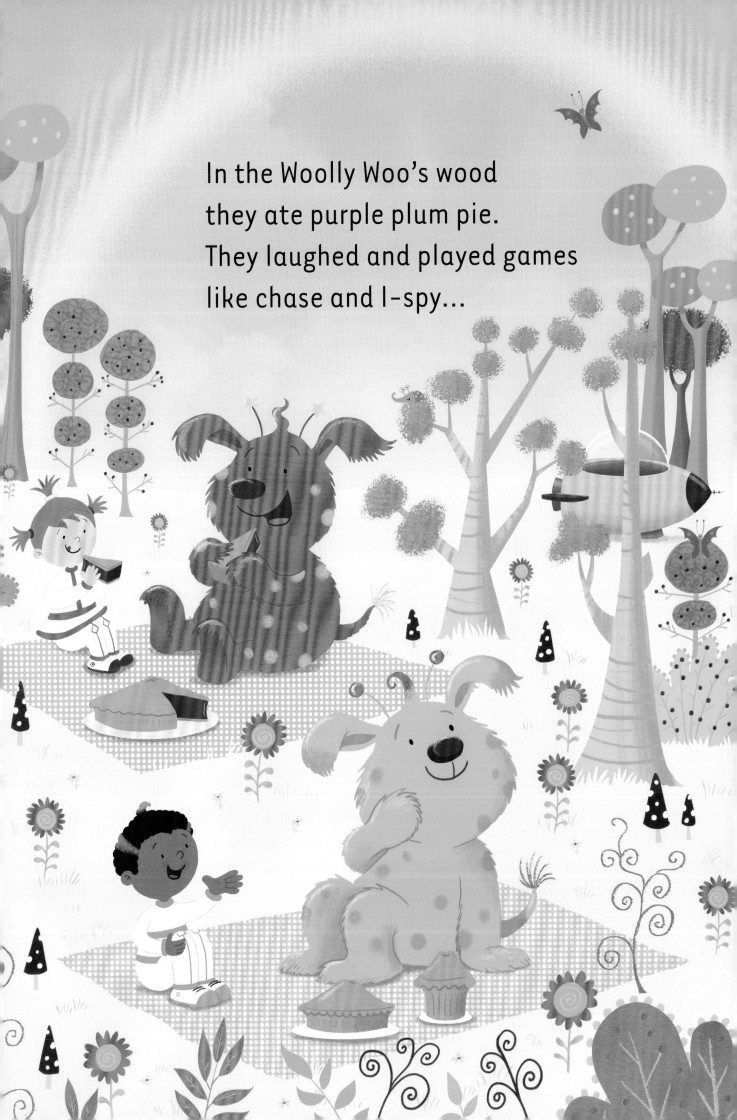

Until yawning, they waved and
got ready to fly…

The rocket stopped DEAD.

They drifted and turned in that dark, empty place… a twirling and whirling…

BLACK HOLE
IN SPACE!

The rocket raced round.
The rocket flew

DOWN DOWN DOWN DOWN

near the hole,
so far from the stars
they would never be found,
by BIG ships and SMALL ships,
or FAST ships and SLOOOW ships,
or LOUD ships and ssSSSH! ships
or even...

"PIRATES FROM MARS!" yelled Blip.

"I know what to do!"

Then straight up they flew!

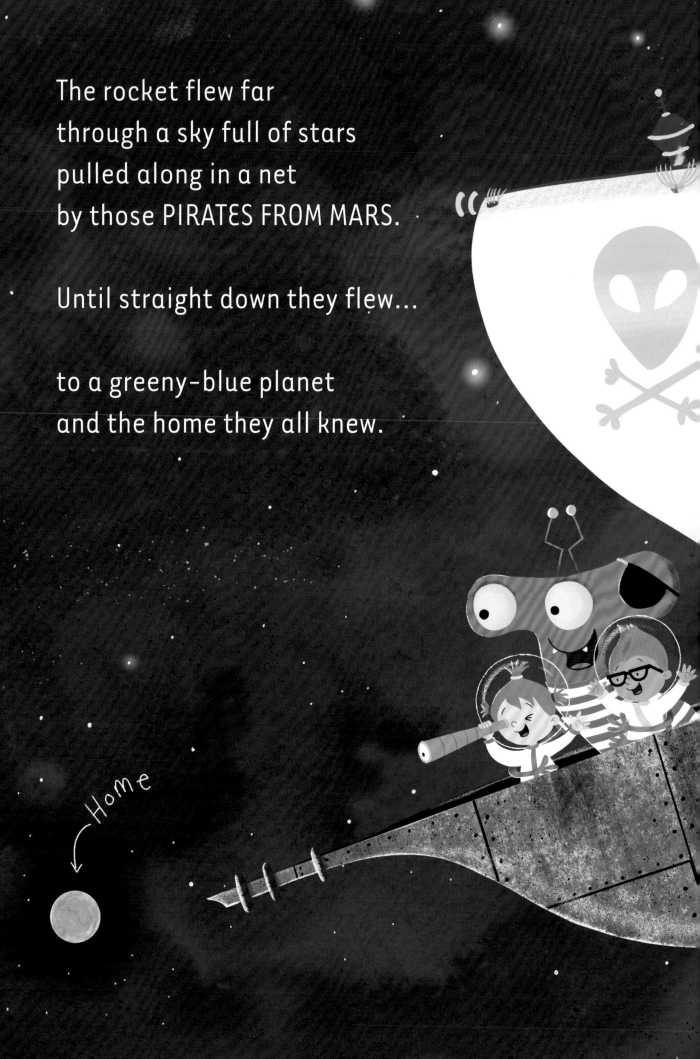

The rocket flew far
through a sky full of stars
pulled along in a net
by those PIRATES FROM MARS.

Until straight down they flew...

to a greeny-blue planet
and the home they all knew.

Home

Just past the moon,
in deep, darkest space
there's a greeny-blue planet
and a snuggly-bug place
called home.

"Let's explore!
Rocket ready!
Press the button...
Whee!" said Eddy
"Whoosh!" said Freddy.
"Whoopee!" said Blip.

Addy Farmer has published poetry, *Help! The teachers are coming!*, a chapter book, *Grandad's bench*, and picture books, *Siddharth and Rinki* and *A bagful of stars*. She won a Northern Writer's Award for Outstanding Promise for her teen novel, *The empty girl*.

She has developed story worlds with a start up company and written scripts for Chinese animation. She is currently working on a funny, mid-grade novel about a boy and his invisible rabbit, *Rabbity*.

addyfarmer.com
notesfromtheslushpile.com

Louise Gardner has been working as a professional illustrator for more than twenty five years, and has illustrated over 150 books for children.
Art has always been the main passion in her life, and she loves drawing anything cute, silly or fun.

She especially likes drawing rabbits, cows, elephants, otters and sloths!

louisegardner.com

Dear Nico
love + stars
Louise

The North Lincolnshire Music Hub is delighted to have commissioned this wonderful story book for young children written by Addy Farmer and illustrated by Louise Gardner.

A successful Arts Council England Grants for the Arts funding bid, alongside additional financial support from local Rotary and Lions organisations and generous in kind support from North Lincolnshire Council (including the Music Service, Community Engagement and Family Learning and Arts Development) has made this book possible. Cultural and education staff from North Lincolnshire Council have also given their support to this project. *A Place Called Home* provides enjoyment and inspiration for young children and adults alike as it allows us to race through the stars, explore space, new planets, meet and make new friends, before returning us safely to our "snuggly-bug place called home".

Addy's wonderful story provides many creative openings for art, movement, rhyme, music and song. The Music Hub was delighted therefore to commission Sue Nicholls to write a collection of catchy songs with arrangements by Hilary Miles to facilitate the story's development; also to engage the much acclaimed story-teller Kirsty Mead of Rhubarb Theatre, whose ideas and inspiration have further enhanced the story. Together we have created a fantastic, creative adventure for young children.

Our thanks go to all involved in making this project such a success.

Erica Hardy – Development Officer, Cultural and Education Partnerships (Project Lead)

musichubnorthlincs.co.uk

A PLACE CALLED HOME
This edition published 2018
Text copyright © Addy Farmer, 2018
Illustrations copyright © Louise Gardner, 2018

The right of Addy Farmer and Louise Gardner to be identified as the author and illustrator of
this work has been asserted in accordance with the Copyright, Designs and Patents Act 1988.
All rights reserved. No part of this publication may be reproduced, stored in a retrieval system,
or transmitted in any form or by any means, electronic, mechanical, photocopying, recording
or otherwise, without the prior permission of the publishers.

Produced by Simona Sideri
Printed and bound by mixam.co.uk